THOMAS & FRIENDS

THOMAS and the SNOWY TRACKS

A Random House PICTUREBACK® Book

Random House 🏠 New York

Thomas the Tank Engine & Friends™

CREATED BY BRITT ALLCROFT

Based on the Railway Series by the Reverend W Awdry. © 2012, 2017 Gullane (Thomas) LLC.
Thomas the Tank Engine & Friends and Thomas & Friends are trademarks of Gullane (Thomas) Limited. Thomas the Tank Engine & Friends and Design Is Reg. U.S. Pat. & Tm. Off. All rights reserved. Published in the United States by Random House Children's Books, a division of Penguin Random House LLC, 1745 Broadway, New York, NY 10019, and in Canada by Penguin Random House Canada Limited, Toronto. Originally published in different form as *Snowy Tracks,* in Great Britain by Egmont UK, in 2012. Pictureback, Random House, and the Random House colophon are registered trademarks of Penguin Random House LLC.
randomhousekids.com   www.thomasandfriends.com
ISBN 978-1-5247-1958-6
MANUFACTURED IN CHINA
10 9 8 7 6 5 4 3 2 1
Glitter effects and production: Red Bird Publishing Ltd., U.K.

HiT entertainment

It had snowed all night on the Island of Sodor. When the engines woke in the morning, everything was white. The railway tracks were under a blanket of sparkling white snow, too.

Sir Topham Hatt asked Thomas to deliver firewood to the stations. He told Gordon to deliver trucks to the Docks.

"The snow is slippery, Gordon," he warned. "Take the long way around the hills."

"I'm going *straight* to the Docks," Gordon said, pumping his pistons proudly. "I'm STRONG. I can easily steam over any hill I come to."

But Thomas was worried. He'd listened to Sir Topham Hatt. He knew that snow could be dangerous.

Gordon huffed away. He came to a hill. "It's not too steep for me," he boomed. And up he went without a hitch. But going down the other side, his wheels slipped and slid. . . .

Gordon went faster and faster. Spencer was huffing up the hill toward him.

"Slow down!" Spencer shouted. But Gordon couldn't slow down. He wheeshed past Spencer, spraying him — *splat!* — with slushy snow. On Gordon raced.

Finally, Gordon slowed down. Soon he came to the biggest hill on the island.

"Snow is soft and I am STRONG," he said. "It won't bother me."

But as Gordon pushed upward through the snow, it became a snowball, which grew bigger and bigger. . . .

Thomas came up the hill behind Gordon. "Thank you for clearing the tracks," Thomas said.

But—uh-oh!—the giant snowball had become too big and heavy. It began to push Gordon back down the hill again!

"Watch out, Thomas!" he shouted.

The snowball pushed Gordon backward—faster and faster!

So Thomas chuffed backward faster and faster . . . until Gordon rolled into a siding.

Then—*crash!*—the snowball bashed into Thomas, knocking him right off the rails!

Gordon tried to shunt Thomas and his trucks of firewood back onto the track. But he couldn't do it.

"I'm sorry, Thomas," he puffed sadly. "I'm not strong after all. I'll find Rocky. He's better at this than I am."

Gordon dropped off his trucks at the Docks, where he found Rocky. He shunted Rocky back to Thomas. Rocky used his long crane arm to heave and heave until Thomas was back on the tracks.

Thomas thanked Rocky. "Now I must deliver my firewood," he said. "I'm very late. The station workers will be cold."

"I'll help you," Gordon said. They puffed slowly off through the snow. Together they delivered firewood to all the stations. And when they came to a hill, they were sure to puff around it.